Books should be returned or renewed by the last date
above. Renew by phone **08458 247 200** or online
www.kent.gov.uk/libs

Libraries & Archives

The Mad Scientist Next Door

By Clare De Marco

Illustrated by Rory Walker

FRANKLIN WATTS

LONDON•SYDNEY

Chapter 1

Ella's next door neighbour, Mr Willis, was mean. The other children didn't like playing near his house.

Even cats stayed away from his garden. Ella kept out of his way.

One day, Ella had an emergency. Her little brother Tom's favourite bear had been catapaulted by accident over Mr Willis' fence. Ella had to get it back before bedtime.

Ella fetched the stepladder and put it up against the fence. Peering over, Ella could see Bear. She could also see thick brambles, so she could not climb over.

Suddenly she could see Mr Willis staring at her from a window.

"You'd better come over!" roared Mr Willis.

Nervously, Ella shuffled up the path

to Mr Willis' front door.

The door creaked open.

"Come in then," growled Mr Willis.

Chapter 2

Ella tried to look brave as she walked into
the lounge. In the corner, she could see
Pickles, a cat who belonged to Thea
from number 15.

Then Ella gulped. This wasn't a lounge.
It was a lab!

There were bottles and jars full of brilliant coloured liquids. There were tubes and pistons with balls on the ends pushing in and out of the fantastic bottles.

"WOW!" gasped Ella.

"Don't. Touch. Anything!" barked Mr Willis.

But too late – Ella had just wiggled her finger in a flickering current that was jumping between two bell jars.

There was a blinding flash. The lab flooded with orange light.

Then everything was back as it was before, except it wasn't. Now Ella found herself looking at herself from across the room.

"What on Earth?" she started to say.

But her voice wasn't her voice.

It was the voice of Mr Willis.

Chapter 3

Ella watched as her face started to laugh.

"We've swapped bodies," said her voice.

"I've been trying to do this for years but

I've only ever had cats to practise on before.

Now you're me and I'm you! I get to be a

child again!"

Ella nervously rubbed her prickly chin.

Mr Willis was twirling around the room.

"Now I will skip and jump! Someone else

will do my washing and cook my dinner!"

he sang happily.

"Swap us back!" shouted Ella. "It's not fair!"

"Not likely," scoffed Mr Willis, and with that

he ran past Ella and out the front door.

Ella started to cry. How would she get her

body back? How could she live next door to

her family without them knowing? And how

could they live with Mr Willis?

She looked at Pickles. "So that's why the cats stayed away!" she thought. Then Ella remembered Bear and wondered what Tom would do when he realised Bear had gone.

She cried even harder. Then she smiled. Bear would help Ella get her body back!

Chapter 4

Ella ran into the garden as fast as Mr Willis' creaky knees would let her. She used a rake to hook Bear out from the brambles.

Now she needed to get Tom's attention. Ella climbed the tree at the bottom of the garden. It was hard work in Mr Willis' old body.

Finally she reached a branch high enough to see over the fence. Luckily, Tom was still playing in the sandpit. She could see Mr Willis jumping on her bed through her bedroom window.

19

"Little boy! Tom!
I have your bear!"
shouted Ella.
She waved the bear at
her little brother.

"BEAR!" yelled Tom.
He stretched out his
arm. Then his face
scrunched up and
he started to cry.

Ella saw her mum and Mr Willis come out of the back door.

"MY BEAR!" screamed Tom, wailing louder and louder. He pointed at Ella in the tree.

"Shh, Tom," said Mum. "We'll get Bear back.

Mr Willis, be careful. I'll pop in to fetch Bear."

"No!" cried Ella.

"Excuse me?" said her mother.

"I want Ella to come and get the bear back.

She catapaulted it into my garden and I

want her to apologise!" shouted Ella.

Ella knew she would pay for this but it had
to be better than being Mr Willis.

"Quite right, Mr Willis!" said Mum.

"But Mum," wheedled Mr Willis.

"That's enough from you, Ella!" said her
mother, sternly. "You will go and apologise
to Mr Willis. Then you can bring Bear back."
Mr Willis looked furious.

Chapter Five

Ella didn't waste time. She jumped out of the tree, twisting her ankle as she landed. "Oh well," she thought. "Serves him right – it won't be my ankle soon!"

Ella hopped into the house with Bear.

She left the front door slightly open.

Then she set everything up exactly as it

had been when the swap happened.

There – Pickles was in the corner. The little electric current was still flickering between the two bell jars.

Ella left Bear exactly on the spot where Mr Willis had been standing before. She stood right by the current.

The doorbell rang.

"It's open!" called Ella. "You'll have to come in, I've hurt my ankle."

"In you go!" Ella heard her mother say. Mr Willis shuffled in with Ella's mother behind him.

As Mr Willis reached to pick up Bear, Ella wiggled her finger in the flickering electric current between the jars.

Again, there came the blinding flash.

Then everything was as before.

Ella could hardly bear to open her eyes.

What if it hadn't worked?

Then she felt her mother's hand in her back.

"Hurry up, Ella!"

Ella opened her eyes, and saw Mr Willis,

in Mr Willis' body. She started to laugh.

Mr Willis looked miserable.

"I only wanted to play," he said, sadly.

"Pardon?" said Ella's mum. "And Ella,

I don't know why you're laughing. Mr Willis

now has a bad ankle because of you.

"Don't worry, Mr Willis. Ella will help with your washing and cooking until your ankle heals. That will be her punishment for catapaulting Bear."

Mr Willis ˌted to laugh.

"But Mum!" cried Ella.

First published in 2013 by
Franklin Watts
338 Euston Road
London
NW1 3BH

Franklin Watts Australia
Level 17/207 Kent Street
Sydney
NSW 2000

Text © Clare De Marco 2013
Illustration © Rory Walker 2013

The rights of Clare De Marco to be
identified as the author and Rory Walker
as the illustrator of this Work have been
asserted in accordance with the Copyright,
Designs and Patents Act, 1988.

Series Editor: Melanie Palmer
Editor: Jackie Hamley
Series Advisor: Catherine Glavina
Series Designer: Peter Scoulding

A CIP catalogue record for this book is
available from the British Library.

ISBN 978 1 4451 2643 2 (hbk)
ISBN 978 1 4451 2649 4 (pbk)
ISBN 978 1 4451 2661 6 (library ebook)

Printed in China

Franklin Watts is a division of Hachette
Children's Books, an Hachette UK company.
www.hachette.co.uk